For Anna Barcock,
a true friend,
with love from Emma

First published in Great Britain in 2008 by Orchard Books,
a division of Hachette Children's Books, London

Little, Brown and Company

Hachette Book Group USA
237 Park Avenue, New York, NY 10017
Visit our Web site at www.lb-kids.com

First U.S. Edition: April 2009

Library of Congress Cataloging-in-Publication Data

Dodd, Emma, 1969-
  I don't want a posh dog!/ by Emma Dodd. -- 1st U.S. ed.
      p. cm.
   Summary: A girl describes in rhyming text the types of dogs she does
not want, and finally arrives at a dog that she can call her own.
  ISBN 978-0-316-03390-9
 [1. Stories in rhyme. 2. Dogs--Fiction.] I. Title. II. Title: I don't want
a posh dog!
  PZ8.3.D636Iad 2009
  [E]--dc22
2008002229

10 9 8 7 6 5 4 3 2 1

Printed in Singapore

I don't want a posh dog!

Emma Dodd

LITTLE, BROWN AND COMPANY
Books for Young Readers

New York Boston

I don't
want a
posh dog.

A blow-dry-when-washed dog.

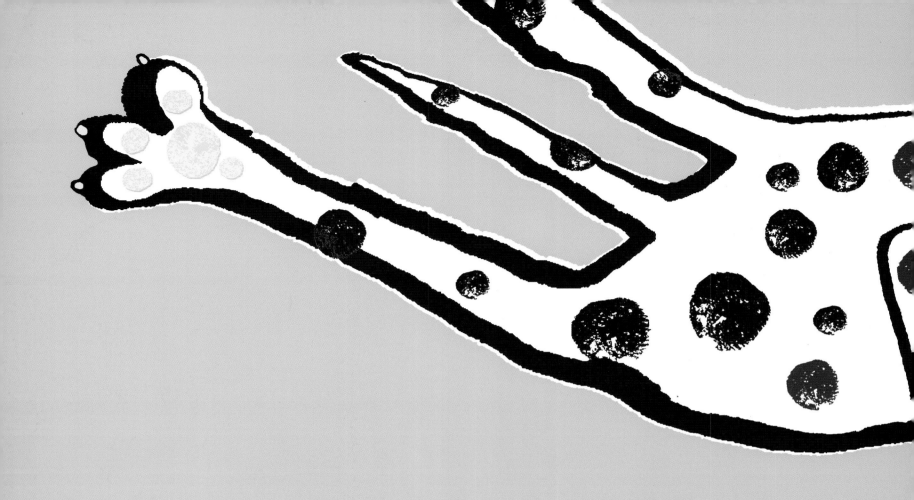

I don't want a bouncy dog.
A jump-up-and-pounce-me dog.

I don't want a snooty dog.

A fancy, attitudey dog.

I don't want
a snappy dog.

A growly,
never-happy
dog.

I don't want a gruff dog.

A grunty, wheezy,
tough dog.

I don't want a speedy dog.

A greedy,

I don't want
an itchy dog.
A scritchy,
scratchy,
twitchy
dog.

I just want a silly dog.
A sweet willy-nilly dog.

A not-too-proud or loud dog.

A know-me-in-the-crowd dog.

An always-ready-to-try dog...

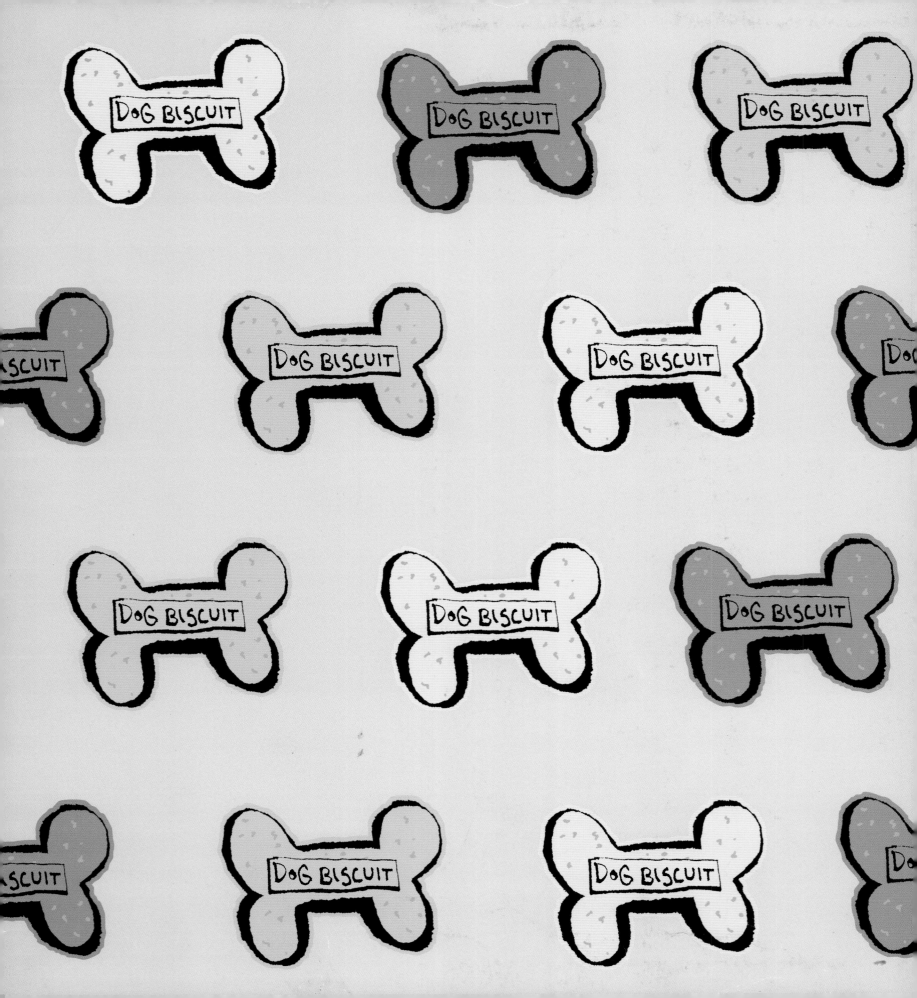